Contents

Klaus Vogel AND THE BAD LADS

David Almond

With illustrations by
Vladimir Stankovic

For Southlands School

Published in 2014 in Great Britain by
Barrington Stoke Ltd
18 Walker Street, Edinburgh, EH3 7LP

www.barringtonstoke.co.uk

This edition adapted by Barrington Stoke Ltd
Published by arrangement with
Walker Books Ltd., London SE11 5HJ

Originally published in *Free?* compiled by
Amnesty International UK.

Text © 2009 David Almond (UK) Ltd
Illustrations © 2014 Vladimir Stankovic

A CIP catalogue record for this book is available
from the British Library upon request

ISBN: 978-1-78112-269-3

Printed in China by Leo

1

We'd been together for years.

We called ourselves the Bad Lads, but it was just a joke. We were mischief-makers, pests and scamps. We never caused proper trouble – at least, not till that autumn. Round about the time we were turning 13. Round about the time Klaus Vogel came.

The Bad Lad regulars were me, Tonto McKenna from Stivvey Court, Dan Digby, and the Spark twins Fred and Frank. We all came from Felling and we all went to St John's. Then there was Joe Gillespie. He was a year or so older than the rest of us, and he kept himself a bit apart, but he was the leader, and he was great.

Joe's hair was long and curled over his collar. He wore faded Levi's, Chelsea boots, Ben Sherman shirts. He had a girlfriend, Teresa Doyle. He used to walk hand in hand with her in Holly Hill Park. I used to dream about being just like Joe. I'd flick my hair back with my hand, wink at girls, put my arm around one of the lads after a specially good stunt. "We done really good, didn't we?" I'd say. "We're really bad, aren't we? Ha ha ha!"

All of us, not just me, wanted to be a bit like

Joe in those days.

2

Most days, after school, we took a ball onto the playing field at Swards Road and put two jumpers down for a goal. We played keep-up and penalties. We practised diving headers, swerves and traps. We played matches with tiny teams and one goal, but we still got carried away by it all just like when we were 8 or 9. We called each other Bestie, Pele, Yashin, and commentated on the moves.

"He's beaten one man, he's beaten two!" we would shout. "Can he do it? *Yeees!* Oh no! Oh, what a save by the Russian in the black top!"

We punched the air when we scored a goal and waved at an invisible roaring crowd. Our voices bounced across the field and over the rooftops. Our breath rose in plumes as the air chilled and the evening came on.

We felt ecstatic, transformed.

Then after a while one of us would see Joe coming out from among the houses, and we'd come back down to the real world.

Most days Joe had a trick or two of his own lined up, but he always made a point of asking what trick we fancied doing next.

Tonto might say, "We could play knocky nine door in Balaclava Street."

Or Frank might go, "Jump through the hedges in Coldwell Park Drive?"

But we'd all just groan at things like that. They were little kids' tricks, and we'd done them tons of times before.

Sometimes there were new ideas. One night we howled like ghosts into Mrs Minto's letterbox. Another time we phoned the police and said an escaped lunatic was chopping up Miss O'Sullivan in her front garden. And another time we tied a piece of string at head height right across Dunelm Terrace.

But the best plans almost always turned out to be Joe's. It was his idea, for instance, to put broken bottles under Mr Tatlock's car tyres, and to dig up the leeks in Albert Finch's allotment.

We went along with Joe, but by the time that autumn came, some of his plans were starting to bother us all.

3

One evening, the sky was glowing red over St Patrick's steeple, and it was clear that none of us had any new tricks to suggest. Joe rubbed his hands together and grinned. He had a rolled-up newspaper stuck into his jeans pocket.

"It's a cold night, lads," he said. "How about a bit of a blaze to warm us up?"

"A blaze?" Tonto said.

"Aye." Joe winked. He rattled a box of matches. "Follow me."

Joe led us up Swards Road and across The Drive and into the narrow lane behind Oak Grove. We stopped in the near darkness under a great over-grown hedge. Joe told us to be quiet and to gather close.

"Just look at the state of this," he whispered.

He put his hand up into the hedge and shook it. Dust and litter and old dead leaves fell out of it. I scratched at something crawling in my hair.

"Would *your* dads let *your* hedge get into a mess like this?" he said.

"No," we answered.

"No," Joe said. "It's just like he is. Crazy and stupid and wild."

"Like who is?" Frank whispered.

"Like him!" Joe said. "Like Useless Eustace!"

Mr Eustace. He lived in the house behind the hedge. He had no family, no pals. He'd been a teacher for a while but he'd given up. Now he spent most of his time stuck inside the house, where he wrote poems, read books, listened to weird music.

"We're gonna burn it down," Joe said.

"Eh?" I said.

"The hedge," Joe said. "Burn it down, teach him a lesson."

The hedge loomed above us against the darkening sky.

"Why?" I asked.

Joe sighed. "Cos it's a mess and cos we're the Bad Lads. And he deserves it."

He unrolled the newspaper and started to shove pages into the hedge. He handed pages to us as well. "Stuff them low down," he said, "so it'll catch better."

I held back. I imagined the roar of the flames, the belching smoke. "I don't think we should," I found myself saying.

The other lads watched as Joe grabbed my collar and glared into my eyes.

"You think too much," he whispered. "You're a Bad Lad. So be a Bad Lad."

Joe finished shoving the paper in. He got the matches out. "Anyway," he said, "he was a bloody conchie, wasn't he?"

Conchie. The word came from before any of us were born. Mr Eustace wouldn't fight in the Second World War. He was against all war – he couldn't attack his fellow man. He was a conscientious objector. My dad and the other lads' dads went off to risk their lives fighting the Germans and the Japanese. But Mr Eustace was sent to jail instead, then they let him out to work on a farm in Durham.

"That was ages back," I said. "He was only doing what he believed in."

"He was a coward and a conchie," Joe said. "And like me dad says – once a conchie ..."

"Don't do it, Joe," I begged.

"You gonna be a conchie too?" he said. "*Are* you?" He looked at all of us. "Are *any* of you going to be conchies?"

"No," we said.

"Good lads." He put his arm round me. "Blame me," he whispered. "I'm the leader. You're only doing what you're told. So do it."

I hated myself, but I shoved my bit of crumpled paper into the hedge with the rest of them.

Mr Eustace suffered when he was a conchie. He had suffered since. My dad said he'd been a decent bloke, but when he'd turned conchie it had ruined his life. He'd never find peace. He should have left this place and started a new life somewhere else, but he never did.

Joe lit a match and held it to the paper. Flames flickered. They started rising fast. Tonto was already backing away down the lane. Fred and Frank were giggling. Dan had disappeared. I cursed. For a moment, I couldn't move.

Then we were all away, running hunched over in the shadows, and the hedge was roaring behind us.

By the time we were back at Swards Road there was a great orange glow over Oak Grove, and smoke was belching up towards the stars.

"Now that," Joe said, "is what I call a proper Bad Lads stunt!"

And no matter what we thought inside, all of us shivered with the thrill of it.

Next morning I went back to the lane. It was black and soaking wet from the ash and the hosepipes. The hedge was just a few black twisted stems. Mr Eustace was in the garden talking to a policeman. He shrugged, shook his head. He caught my eye and I wanted to yell out, 'You're useless! What did you expect? You should have started a new life somewhere else!'

Joe was nowhere in sight but Fred and Frank were grinning from further down the lane. Neighbours had come out, muttering and whispering. None of them suspected anything, of course. They knew us. We were Felling lads. There was no badness in us. Not really.

4

That was the week Klaus Vogel arrived. He was a scrawny little kid from East Germany. The tale was that his dad was a famous singer who'd been hauled off to a prison camp somewhere in Russia. The mother had disappeared – shot, people said. The kid had been smuggled out in the boot of a car.

Nobody knew the full truth, my dad said, not when it had happened so far away and in countries like that. He said we should just be happy we lived in a place like this where we could go about as we pleased.

Klaus stayed in the priest's house next to St Patrick's and he came to our school, St John's. He didn't have a word of English, but he was bright and he learned fast. Soon he could speak a few English words, in a weird Geordie-German accent. It wasn't long before he was even writing a few words in English.

We looked at his book one break.

"How the hell do you *do* it?" Dan asked.

Klaus raised his hands. He didn't know how to explain. "I just ..." he began, and he scribbled hard and fast. "Like so," he said.

We saw the jagged English words mixed up with what had to be German.

"What is it?" Tonto said.

"Is story of my *vater*," Klaus said. "My father. It must be ..." He frowned into the air, seeking the word.

"Must be *told*," I said.

"*Danke*. Thank you." He nodded and his eyes widened. "It must be told. *Ja!* Aye!"

And we all laughed at the way he used the Tyneside word.

Outside school Klaus talked with his feet. He played the kind of football we could only dream of – overhead kicks, sudden body swerves, curling free kicks. He was tiny, clever, tough. We gasped in admiration. When he played, he lost himself in the game, and all his troubles seemed to fall away.

"What'll we call you?" Frank asked.

Klaus frowned. "Klaus Vogel," he said.

"No," Frank said. "Your football name. I'm Pele. You are ..."

Klaus pondered. He glanced around, as if to check who was listening. "Müller," he murmured. *"Ja!* Gerd Müller!"

Then he grinned, twisted, dodged a tackle, swerved the ball into the corner of the invisible net and waved to the invisible crowd.

All the lads yelled, "Yeah! Well done, Müller!"

5

The first time Klaus Vogel met Joe was a few weeks after he'd arrived. Since the hedge fire, things had gone quiet. Joe spent most of his time with Teresa Doyle. We'd seen him a couple of times, leaning on a fence on Swards Road watching us play, but he hadn't come across. Now here he was, strolling onto the field in the icy November dusk. I moved to Klaus's side.

"He's called Joe," I whispered. "He's OK."

"So this is the famous Klaus Vogel," Joe said.

Klaus shrugged.

Joe smiled. "And your dad's the famous singer, eh?" he said. "The *op-era* singer."

"Aye," Klaus said.

"Giz a song, then."

"What?" said Klaus.

"He must've taught you, eh?" Joe said. "And we like a bit of *op-era* here, don't we, lads? Go on, giz a song." Joe opened his mouth wide and stretched his hand out like he was singing to a concert hall. "Go on," he said. "You're in a free country now, you know. Sing up!"

Klaus stared at him.

I wanted to say, "Don't do it," but Klaus stepped away, closer to Joe. He took a deep breath and started to sing. His voice rang out across the field. It was weird, like the music that drifted from Mr Eustace's house. We heard the loveliness in it. How could he *do* such things?

But Joe bent over, struggling with laughter. Then he waved his hands to bring Klaus to a halt.

Klaus stopped and stared again. "You do not like?" he asked.

Joe wiped the tears of laughter from his eyes. "Aye, aye," he said. "It's brilliant, son."

Then Joe opened his own mouth and started to sing, a wobbly high-pitched imitation of Klaus. He looked at us and we all started to laugh with him.

"Mebbe we're just not ready for it, eh, lads?" Joe said.

"Mebbe we're not," Frank muttered. He turned his eyes away.

Klaus looked at us too. Then he just shrugged again. "So. I will go home," he said.

"No," said Joe. "You can't."

"Can't?" Klaus asked.

"We can't let you." Joe grinned. He winked. "We got to see if he passes the test, don't we, lads? We got to make him one of the Bad Lads." He showed his teeth like he was a great beast, then he smiled. "It's extra important when you consider where he comes from, eh?"

"What you mean?" Klaus asked.

"From *Germany*," Joe said. "Not so long ago we'd have been wanting to kill you. You'd've been wanting to kill us."

Joe raised his hand like he had a gun in it and pointed it at Klaus. He pulled an invisible trigger. Then he smiled. "It's nowt, son," he said. "Just some carry-on. What'll it be, lads? Knocky nine door in Balaclava Street? Jumping the hedges in Coldwell Park Drive?"

"The hedges," I said. I put my hand on Klaus's arm. "It's OK," I whispered. "We're just messing about. And it's on your way home."

So Klaus came with us. We cut across the lanes to Coldwell Park Drive and slipped into the gardens behind. Then Joe led us and we charged over the back lawns and over the hedges while dogs howled and people yelled at us to cut it out. We streamed out, giggling, onto Felling Bank. Joe held us in a quick huddle and said it was just like the old days. He put his arm round Klaus.

"Ha!" he said. "You're a proper Bad Lad now, Herr Vogel. You're one of us!"

Then we started to run our separate ways along the shadows.

Klaus caught my arm. "Why?" he said.

"Why what?" I asked.

"Why do we do *that*?" he said. "Why we do what Joe says?"

"It's not like that," I said. I stopped. "It's ..." But my voice felt all caught up inside me, like it couldn't find words.

"Is *what*?" Klaus said.

He held my arm like he really wanted to understand. But I had no answers. Klaus shrugged his shoulders, shook his head, walked away.

6

Klaus kept away from the Bad Lads for a while.
He scribbled in his book, writing his story. He
sang out loud in music lessons. He dazzled
everyone with his football skills in Games.

There were rumours that the body of
his mother had turned up. The whole school
prayed for East Germany, for Russia, for Klaus
Vogel and his family.

One day after school, I came upon Klaus.
He was walking under the trees on Watermill
Lane. He walked fast, swinging his arms,
singing softly.

"Klaus!" I said. "What you doing?"

"I am being free!" he said. "My father said that one day I would walk as a free man. I would walk and sing and show the world that I am free. So I do it. Look!"

He strode in circles, swinging his arms again.

"Do I look like I am free?" he asked.

"Yes," I laughed. "Of course you do."

He laughed too. "Ha! As I walk I think of him in his cell. I think of her."

"They would be proud of you," I said.

"Would they?" he said.

"Yes."

Klaus laughed again, a bitter laugh. "And as I walk I think of my friends here," he said. "I think of you, I think of Joe."

"Of Joe?" I said.

"*Ja!* Him!"

"You think too much, Klaus," I told him. "Come and play football, will you? Come and be Gerd Müller."

And he sighed and shrugged. OK.

It was getting dark. Frost already glistened on the field. The stars were like a field of vivid frost above. Klaus played with more skill and passion than ever. We watched him in wonder. He ran with the ball at his feet, he flicked it into the goal, he leaped with joy, he danced to the crowd.

Then Joe was there. His footsteps crackled across the grass. He had a small rucksack on his back.

"Herr Vogel," he said. "Nice to see you again."

He stepped closer and put his arm round Klaus. "Sorry to hear about ..." He held up his hand, as if to stop his own words. "Our thoughts are with you, son."

He turned to the rest of us. "Now, lads. It's a fine night for a Bad Lads stunt."

You could tell it was almost over with us and Joe. We were reluctant to gather around him. Our smiles were forced when he told us he had the perfect trick. But he was tall and strong. He smelled of aftershave, he wore a black Ben Sherman shirt, black jeans, black Chelsea boots. We hadn't broken free of him yet.

Joe drew us into a huddle. He smiled and
told us we'd always been the Bad Lads and we'd
keep on being the Bad Lads, wouldn't we?

No one said 'no'. No one objected when
he told us to follow. I think I hesitated for
a moment, but Klaus came to my side and
whispered, "You will not go? But you must. We
must all follow our leader, mustn't we?"

And Klaus stepped ahead, and I followed.

Joe led us to The Drive, towards the lane
behind Oak Grove.

"Not again," I sighed.

"It's like me dad says," Joe said. "Eustace
should've been drove out years back." He
turned to Klaus. "It's local stuff, son. I bet

your lot had better ways of dealing with the Eustaces than we ever had."

Klaus just shrugged.

"Anyway, lads, it's just a bit of fun this time," Joe said. He opened his rucksack, took out a box of eggs. "Here, one each. Hit a window for 100 points."

A couple of the lads giggled. They took their eggs. Joe held the box out to me. I hesitated. Klaus took one and looked at me. So I took an egg and held it in my hand.

Joe smiled and patted Klaus's back. "Good Bad Lad, Herr Vogel," he murmured.

Klaus laughed his bitter laugh again.

"*Nein*," he said. "I am not a good Bad Lad. I am Klaus Vogel."

He stepped towards Joe.

"I do not like you," he said. "I do not like the things you make others do."

"Oh! You do *not like?*" Joe said.

"*Nein.*"

Joe laughed. He mocked the word – "*Nein! Nein! Nein!*" – as he stamped the ground and gave a Nazi salute. He grabbed Klaus by the collar, but Klaus didn't step back.

"You could crush me in a moment," he said. "But I am not … *ängstlich.*"

"Scared," I said.

"*Ja!* I am not scared. *Ich bin frei!*"

"Ha! *Frei. Frei.*"

"He is free," I said. And in that moment, I knew that Klaus was free. Despite the fact his father was in prison. Despite the fact his mother had died. Despite the fact Joe's fist was gripping his collar. He had said 'no'. He was free.

Joe snarled and drew his fist back. I found myself reaching out. I caught the fist in mid-air.

"No," I said. "You can't do that."

"*What?*"

"I said no!"

7

Joe thumped us both that night, in the lane behind Mr Eustace's house. We fought back, but he was tall and strong and there was little we could do against his anger. Tonto and the others had disappeared.

Afterwards I walked home with Klaus through the frosty starlit night. We were sore and we had blood on our faces, but soon we were swinging our arms.

"Do I look like I am free?" I said.

Klaus laughed. "*Ja! Yes! Aye!*"

And he began to sing and I tried to join in.

A couple of days later Klaus came with me to Mr Eustace's house. I knocked at the door and Mr Eustace opened it.

"I burned down your hedge," I said.

He peered at me. "Did you now?" he said.

I chewed my lips. Music was playing. Beyond Mr Eustace the hallway was lined with books.

"I'm sorry," I said. "I was wrong."

"Yes, you were," he said.

I felt so clumsy, so stupid.

"This is Klaus Vogel," I said. "He is a writer, a footballer, a singer."

"Then he is a civilised man," Mr Eustace told me. "Perhaps you can learn from him."

I nodded. I was about to turn and lead Klaus away, but Mr Eustace said, "Why don't you come inside?"

We followed him in. There were books everywhere. In the living room there was an open notebook on a desk with an uncapped fountain pen lying upon it. The writing in the book was in the shape of poetry.

Mr Eustace stood at the window and waved at the ruins of the hedge outside. "Is that how you wish the world to be?" he asked me.

"No," I answered.

"No."

He made us tea. There were fig rolls and little cakes. He spoke a few words to Klaus in German, and Klaus gasped with pleasure. Then Mr Eustace put another record on. Opera. High sweet voices flowed together and filled the house with their sound.

"Mozart!" Klaus said.

"Yes."

Klaus joined in. His voice rang out. Mr
Eustace closed his eyes and smiled.

Our books are tested
for children and young people by
children and young people.

Thanks to everyone who consulted on
a manuscript for their time and effort in
helping us to make our books better
for our readers.